Written & Illustrated by
JENNIFER LINK

Patches & Buttons

Outskirts Press, Inc.
http://www.outskirtspress.com

ISBN: 978-1-4787-3073-6

Outskirts Press and the "OP" logo are trademarks belonging to Outskirts Press, Inc.

PRINTED IN THE UNITED STATES OF AMERICA

This Book Belongs to:

_____

Buttons is afraid of loud noises it hurts his ears! **"Bang Boom"**! He quickly hops under the bed.

Patches the dog spots him and pokes her big fluffy head under the bed to bark at Buttons.

This makes Buttons very afraid so he hops quickly away into the bathroom behind the towels.

Whoosh! Whoosh!
Buttons could hear the
bathtub filling up. It
was time for Patches to
take a bath.

All of the splashing sounds made Buttons so afraid, that he could not move.

After Patches was done with her bath, little Buttons was able to safely hop away through the living room.

Vroom! Vroom! went the vacuum cleaner! Oh no! thought Buttons another loud noise, I just want a quiet place to nap!

Thump!

Thump! Thump! Thump!
went Buttons back legs!
Bunnies do this when
they feel scared or if
there is danger.

Buttons hopped down the hall to his bunny cage after the scary vacuum cleaner was turned off!

He loved his bed it was safe and no one would bother him in there. Buttons laid down and cleaned his ears and face.

Ruff! Ruff! He heard the big dog Patches then he saw her coming towards the cage! Buttons was scared of the fluffy dog!

Oh no! thought Buttons
I need to hide!

Patches stopped slowly
at the bunny cage carrying
what looked like a small toy.

Patches pushed the stuffed elephant toy towards Buttons.

Buttons lifted up his head and was curious but still a little afraid and not ready to leave the cage.

Buttons crawled slowly to the door and picked up the small little elephant with his mouth. He realized that Patches just wanted to play and wasn't that scary after all.

Patches slowly put her fluffy head into Buttons cage and touched noses knowing now that they would be great friends.

CPSIA information can be obtained
at www.ICGtesting.com
Printed in the USA
BVXC01n0913090614
355606BV00001B/1